Algy's Amazing Adventures
AT
SEA

Look out for

Algy's Amazing Adventures
in the Jungle

Algy's Amazing Adventures
in the Arctic

Algy's Amazing Adventures

AT

SEA

Kaye Umansky

Illustrated by
Richard Watson

Orion
Children's Books

First published in Great Britain in 2014
by Orion Children's Books
a division of the Orion Publishing Group Ltd
Orion House
5 Upper Saint Martin's Lane
London WC2H 9EA
An Hachette UK company

1 3 5 7 9 10 8 6 4 2

The Orion Publishing Group's policy is to use papers that
are natural, renewable and recyclable products and made
from wood grown in sustainable forests. The logging and
manufacturing processes are expected to conform to the
environmental regulations of the country of origin.

A catalogue record for this book is available
from the British Library.

ISBN 978 1 4440 0689 6

Printed and bound in China

www.orionbooks.co.uk

To George

Contents

Chapter One

This is Algy. He lives in an ordinary house in an ordinary street. At the bottom of his garden is an ordinary shed.

But . . . in that shed is
something exciting. A loose
plank. And behind that plank is . . .

Another world!

This is Cherry. She lives next door. When Algy goes on adventures, so does Cherry.

This is Brad, Cherry's little brother. He likes jumping, singing and eating sweets. He likes adventures too.

It was a cold, grey day. Algy
was in the mood for an adventure.

"Where are you going?" asked
his mum.

"Out in the garden," said Algy.
"Put your coat on. And wear
your new scarf," said his mum.

Algy frowned. He didn't like his new scarf. Aunty Sue had made it. It was too bright.

"I don't need it," said Algy.

"You do," said his mum. "It's cold."

"I don't like it," said Algy.

"It's a lovely scarf," said his mum. "Wear it."

So Algy wore it, because he had to.

When Algy got to the shed,
the door was already open.

"Hurry up," came Cherry's
voice. "We've been waiting ages."

Algy stepped inside.

Cherry was standing in front of the loose plank. Brad was with her, bouncing around and waving a carrot.

"Wow!" said Cherry. "That's a bright scarf."

"I know," said Algy.

"Never mind," said Cherry. "Let's see what's behind the plank today."

Brad pushed the plank. It fell outwards, and through the gap was . . .

"The *sea!*" shouted Cherry. "It's the *sea!*"

Chapter Two

A stretch of golden sand led down to a sparkling blue ocean.

Brad dropped his carrot and wriggled through the gap. Algy picked it up and put it in his pocket, because you shouldn't drop litter.

"Wait, Brad!" shouted Cherry. "We're coming!"

Algy didn't like the sea. He had only been four times.

The first time, he'd dropped his ice cream.

The second time, a seagull had stolen his sandwich.

The third time, his cousin
Dawn had thrown sand in his
eye.

The last time, a wave had knocked him over and he'd swallowed so much sea water that he was sick.

"Come on, Algy!" shouted
Cherry. "Hurry up! We're playing
pirates! We're going to sea!"
Algy pretended not to hear.

Palm trees grew thickly around the shed. There were banana trees too.

Algy was about to pick a banana when he heard a voice say, "Hello, George!"

Algy looked up in surprise.
Staring down at him, from a
huge leaf, was a parrot!

Chapter Three

The parrot's feathers were the same colours as Algy's scarf. It had a yellow head, red wings and a long, green tail.

Algy didn't like birds much.
Geese made him nervous.
Pigeons were pests. Seagulls stole
sandwiches.

But he'd never met a parrot
before.

"Hello, George!" said the parrot again.

"I'm not George," said Algy. "I'm Algy."

"George!" said the parrot. "Georgy-Porgy!"

"Oh," said Algy. "*You're* George. Hello."

Suddenly, George darted
forward and grabbed Algy's scarf!
"Hey!" shouted Algy.
Algy pulled. George
pulled too.

There was a tearing sound.

Algy won in the end. But now there was a huge hole in the middle of his scarf. Mum wouldn't be pleased.

George hopped onto Algy's shoulder. He said, "Got a bite, matey?"

Algy couldn't believe it. He had a real live talking parrot on his shoulder!

Maybe he could take George home. He could say he'd found him in the garden.

He would teach him to say "Algy". He would take George to school and everybody would love him.

"Got a bite?" said George. "Biscuit?"

"No biscuit," said Algy. He reached into his pocket. "I've got this, though. A carrot for a parrot. Want it?"

George wanted it all right.
The carrot was gone in two huge
bites.

Then he looked Algy in the eye
and said, "Thankee, matey."

Algy thought George was the
best bird ever.

Chapter Four

Algy couldn't wait to show his new pet to the others. He hurried towards the beach, with George on his shoulder.

Cherry was picking up
shells and Brad was building a
sandcastle by some rocks.

"Come on, George," said Algy.
"Let's say hello to my friends."

"Hello, George," said George.

"No," said Algy. "That's your name. You have to say, 'Hello, Cherry and Brad . . .'"

He stopped.

There was something on the horizon.

A huge sailing ship! And fluttering from the top mast was . . .

The Skull and Crossbones!

Pirates!

Algy gasped. He ducked under the trees.

To his horror, he saw a small boat appear from behind the rocks.

Three ragged, mean-looking men jumped out and splashed ashore.

In a flash, Cherry and Brad
were surrounded!

"*Arrrk,*" said George.
"Shush, George," said Algy. "No
talking. I'm trying to think."

Algy's mind was racing. The trees grew along the beach. Maybe, if he stayed in the shadows, he could get close and find out what was going on.

"Right, George," he whispered. "Let's go."

Algy crept towards the pirates and crouched behind a tall palm tree. He could hear them talking now.

George nibbled his ear and muttered, "Biscuit?"

"No," whispered Algy. "Sssh!"

"So," boomed the pirate in the hat, "for the last time, what are you doing on my island?"

"S-sorry," gulped Cherry. "We didn't know it was private."

"Well, it is. Redbush Isle. Named after me, Captain Redbush. What's that on yer face?"

He reached out and snatched
Cherry's glasses. He held them to
his eye.

"Make you see better, do they?
Is that it? Help you find things?"
he said.

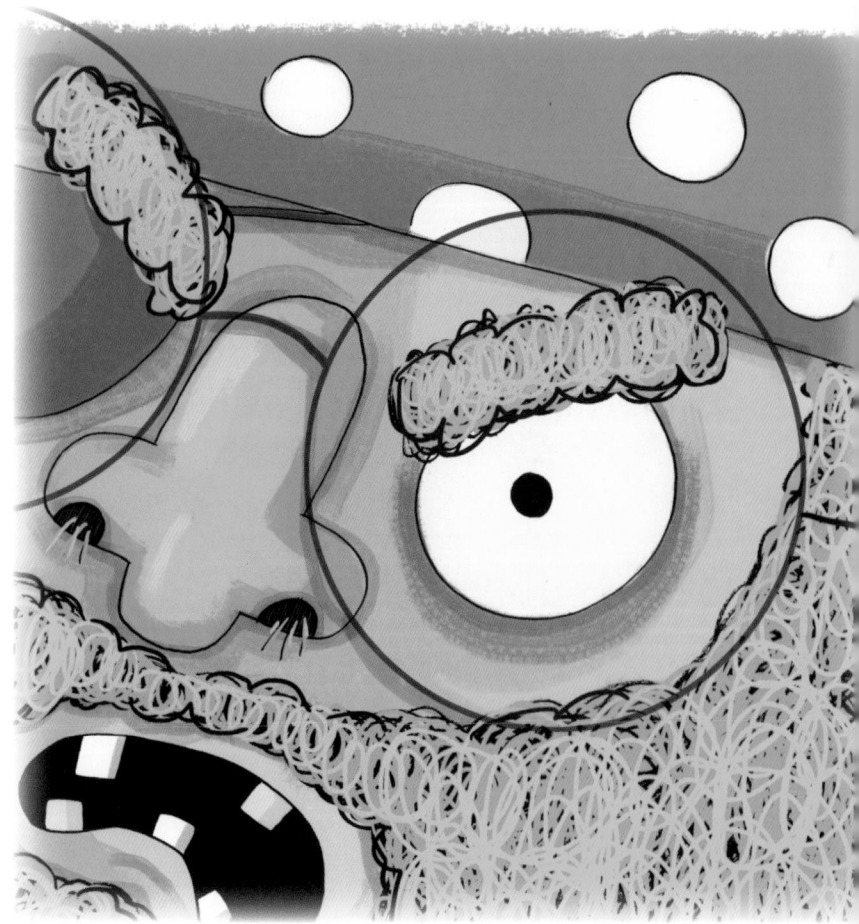

"Yes," said Cherry. "Can I have them back, please?"

"No," growled Captain Redbush. "I be lookin' for somethin'."

The bald pirate grabbed Brad's red cap and tried it on. It didn't fit and just sat on top of his round head.

"Funny!" said Brad, and giggled.

But Captain Redbush wasn't laughing. He was gazing through Cherry's glasses and frowning.

And now he was looking in Algy's direction!

Algy ducked lower.

"No good," growled the Captain. He threw Cherry's glasses into the sand. "Not a sign. Let's get our prisoners back to the ship."

If Algy didn't do something quickly, Cherry and Brad would be taken to sea by pirates and he would never see them again!

With George on his shoulder, Algy raced over the sand and into the water.

"STOP!" he shouted.

Chapter Five

Captain Redbush stopped. He looked round and stared at Algy, his face like thunder.

Algy opened his mouth. He tried to say, "Leave my friends alone!" But nothing came out. Cold water swirled around his knees.

And then –"*Arrrrrk!*" squawked George. He flapped his wings. "*Arrrrrrrk!*"

To Algy's amazement, a huge grin spread across the Captain's face.

"George!" he shouted.

"Georgie-Porgy!" screeched
George. He flapped across and
landed on the Captain's shoulder.

"Ah, George!" cried the Captain.
"Where have ye been? I've been
looking everywhere for you."

George said, "Got a biscuit?"

The small pirate jumped out of the boat and held out a hand to Cherry.

The bald pirate lifted Brad onto his shoulders. All of them came wading ashore.

Soon they were standing on firm, dry sand.

"Thankee, lad," Captain Redbush boomed. "Thought I'd lost him. Ah, George! What would I have done without ye?"

"Best make for the ship, Cap'n," said the bald pirate.

Algy looked at George sadly. He wouldn't be taking him home after all. He wouldn't be teaching him to say "Algy" or taking him to school either.

"Goodbye, George," he said.

George looked at him. Then, very clearly, he said, "Carrot for a parrot! *Ark!*"

"That's a new one, Cap'n," said the bald pirate. "Where did he get that from?"

"Me," said Algy happily. "He got it from me."

Chapter Six

That night, Algy lay in bed, thinking about the adventure. Like all his trips to the sea, there had been bad bits.

Cherry's glasses were even more scratched than usual. That was bad.

Then there was his holey scarf. He'd got into trouble about that.

"It's ruined," said his mum. "It looks as if it's been attacked by a crocodile."

"Parrot," said Algy, not thinking. *"What?"*

"I – um – wondered if Aunty Sue could knit me a parrot? From the wool? It's the right colours."

"Why not ask?" said his mum.

So Algy asked. Aunty Sue sounded a bit surprised but said she would give it a go.

Now, that was good.

Algy put the scarf next to his head on the pillow and went to sleep.